T. V. Harper

Electro-Plating Made Easy

The silver plater's handbook - a clear and comprehensive treatise on the

art of gold, silver and nickel plating

T. V. Harper

Electro-Plating Made Easy
The silver plater's handbook - a clear and comprehensive treatise on the art of gold, silver and nickel plating

ISBN/EAN: 9783337391805

Printed in Europe, USA, Canada, Australia, Japan

Cover: Foto ©Andreas Hilbeck / pixelio.de

More available books at **www.hansebooks.com**

ELECTRO-PLATING MADE EASY.

THE

ver Plater's Hand-Book

A CLEAR AND COMPREHENSIVE TREA-
TISE ON THE ART OF

ıD, SILVER AND NICKEL PLATING,

— EITHER —

VITH OR WITHOUT THE AID OF THE ELECTRIC CURRENT.

By T. V. HARPER.

COLUMBUS, OHIO:
PUBLISHED BY THE AUTHOR.
1883.

INTRODUCTION.

In the preparation of this little work, we have endeavored to make everything as plain and comprehensive as possible, by avoiding as far as practicable all technical terms and names that are thoroughly understood only by those having a fair knowledge of chemistry and its application to electro–metallurgical operations, which it is fair to presume, is not possessed by more than one out of a hundred persons, and as this book is intended more particularly for the practical benefit of the masses, we have adopted the language, and style of expression, best calculated, we think, to supply a want in the field of popular, and scientific literature, heretofore so sadly neglected. At the same time the experienced electro–plater will find herein, facts which will prove not only interesting, but instructive to him.

The history of the art of electro–metallurgy dates far back in the seventeenth century, but not much progress was made in practical application of the then limited knowledge of the art in plating articles in a substantial manner, until sometime after the discovery of voltaic or chemical electricity, which occurred in the year 1799.

The first seven years of the eighteenth century, were fruitful in important discoveries in the art. In 1800 water was first decomposed into its two constituent gases, by means of the voltaic battery, and shortly afterwards it was discovered that silver, in contact with another, and a more positive metal, received a firmly adherent deposit of copper, when placed in a solution of that metal.

In the years of 1804 and 1805, it was first noticed, that when a current of electricity was passed through a solution of sulphate of copper, or nitrate of silver, by means of silver, or platinum wires, the metal held in solution was deposited upon the wire connected with zinc pole of the battery. About a year later, gold was first successfully deposited by means of the electric current, and it was then first noticed, that the anode (or the pole or plate,) by which the electric current entered the solution was slowly dissolved, although it is not clearly shown that any advantage was taken of this fact at that time. This seems strange when we take into consideration the importance of the discovery, which plays so prominent a part in all electro-plating operations.

From this time, until after the year 1831, when magneto-electricity was discovered by Faraday, but little was done in the way of advancing the art of electro-metallurgy.

In the year 1834, Faraday conducted a number of experiments, and discovered among other things, that the amount of salt in a solution decomposed by the electric current, was in direct proportion to the quantity of electricity, and that the quantity of electricity generated in a battery, depended upon the size of the plates the intensity of the current, or its power of overcoming resistence, depending upon the number of cells in circuit.

In the year 1836, it was noticed that the copper pole of a battery somewhat similar to the present Daniell battery, became heavily coated with metallic copper, which constantly increased in thickness, and also that this deposit when removed, presented a faithful outline of the original copper plate, every line and scratch, however fine, being faithfully reproduced.

In the years 1837 and 1839, it occurred to several parties that this fact might be taken advantage of in the reproduction of copper plates, steel engravings, etc., and a great many experiments were conducted with this end in view. One experimentalist had occasion to use a small strip of copper, in a sulphate of copper solution, in conducting one of his experiments, and not having a strip of sheet copper convenient, attached a large copper coin to a wire, and immersed it in the solution, where it remained in circuit for quite a while, and received a heavy deposit of copper. Finally one day while conducting another experiment, it became necessary for him to use the wire attached to the coin, and while removing it he detached a large piece of the deposited copper, and at once observed that it was an exact mold of that portion of the coin, every line, and letter being reproduced with remarkable fidelity.

In the year 1840, the art of electro plating with gold and silver received a fresh impetuous, by the discovery of the suitability of alkaline solutions, and the hitherto unprecedented success attending their use. Great difficulty was still experienced in obtaining a good and firmly adherent deposit upon articles of brittania metal, which was finally remedied, by first coating the articles with copper.

From this time forward, the art has been making rapid strides towards perfection, but in this age of progress and invention, who can gainsay the assertion that, perhaps, it is still in its infancy. So numerous are the wonderful inventions, and startling discoveries, that the more conservative would hesitate, at drawing the boundarly line beyond which inventive genius and scientific research may not proceed.

It would seem to the practical electro plater that there is but little room or necessity for improvement in gold and silver plating solutions, as they are now about all that could be desired.

It is with the electro-deposition of other more obscure metals and metalloids that the fields of scientific research lay invitingly open, the elec-trolysis of carbon being all the more interesting from the fact that it may probably result in the artificial formation of the diamond which, as the reader perhaps knows, is but pure crystalized carbon.

One great obstacle in the way of much research in the way of electro deposition of carbon is difficulty experienced in obtaining solutions containing carbon that are conductors of electricity. The fused or melted carbonates are about the only liquids that have been used with any degree of success so far.

With the melted carbonates of potash and sodium a black and very hard deposit of carbon has been obtained.

The melted carbonate of sodium (washing soda) is, perhaps, the best mixture that has been tried as yet, it being a fair conductor of electricty, and yields a better deposit of carbon than any of the other mixtures.

In conclusion we would say that a strict observance of the rules and formulas contained in this book will be productive of the best of results. Much pains have been taken to give the reader the benefit of all the later discoveries in the art, and the language of the book so adapted that those with but a limited education may easily understand.

GENERAL INFORMATION.

All the vessels used in containing the different solutions, should be of glass, stone, or enameled ware; glass ware being preferred for operations on the small scale. Their size should be adapted to the number and size of the articles to be plated, but for convenience sake we would suggest, that they be capable of containing at least a gallon. They should be kept in a well ventilated room, and where the light can not fall directly upon them. The different acids, and other necessary chemicals, should be kept in well stoppered bottles, and placed carefully out of the reach of meddling hands, as many of them are the most violent poisons, and some of them are capable of producing almost instan death; and others, when mixed, producing the most powerful explosives. Too much care can not be observed in this respect, as many are the sad, and fatal results, of an incautious manner in

the handling of dangerous chemicals, or care-
lessly leaving them where unthoughtful hands
may bring about the most disastrous conse-
quences.

Articles to be re-plated, should first have
the old deposit removed, either by the aid of
different chemicals, which will be mentioned
further along, or by filing and scraping, or
scouring with emery paper. When removed by
means of acids, the metal may be re covered
with but small loss, and where the operation is
carefully conducted, with no loss at all, and used
over again; where a great deal of re plating
is done this is quite an important item in the
economical management of the business.

The prevailing opinion that electro-plating
is necessarily a very expensive operation, is er-
roneous, although we confess that the high
prices at which plated goods are usually sold,
would tend to further that impression, and often
when the purchaser has used the articles a short
time, and worn off the thin plating, thus exposing the baser metal underneath, he would
naturally conclude that what little precious
metal there was there, had been deposited at
great expense.. But where the business is con-

ducted economically, and understandingly, the
total expense is but a very small percentnge
over the intrinsic value of the metal deposited;
as an electro plating solution once properly
made, and then carefully managed, will last for
years, or until it becomes so clogged up with
impurities set free by the dissolving of the anode,
that it will no longer deposit pure metal, and for
this reason, great care should be taken in the
selection of anodes, in order to obtain them as
free as possible from all impurities.

Anodes of silver generally contain traces of
copper, and those of gold contain traces of both
silver and copper, which being dissolved in the
solution and deposited, greatly change the color
and appearance of the articles. When not in
use, the vessels containing the depositing solutions should be carefully covered over to prevent accidents by poisoning, and also to keep
out the dust, and other foreign substances which
might be accidently introduced.

The habit some platers have of dipping
the hands in the solutions to recover articles
that become detached from their supporting
wires, is a very dangerous one to say the least of
it, as some of the poison is apt to be absorbed

through the pores of the skin, or by getting into cuts, or even slight abrasions of the skin, cause troublesome and dangerous sores. The way to recover articles accidentally dropped in the solution, is by means of a wooden spoon or a bent wire.

PREPARING ARTICLES TO BE PLATED.

All articles to be plated must first be made scrupulously clean, in order to obtain a good firm deposit. A great many failures may be attributed to the neglect of this very important step. They should first be filed or scraped, or otherwise made as smooth as possible, then immersed for a short time, in a strong and hot solution of potash, (concentrated lye) and then rinsed well in clean water.

A very good scraper can be easily made by grinding down the sides of a three cornered file until it is perfectly smooth, and finishing up on an oil stone, thus leaving three sharp cutting edges. Articles that have been soldered, must not be allowed to remain long in the potash solution, or a portion of the tin contained in the solder will be dissolved, and deposited on the articles, should they be copper or brass, and blacken them. Articles of copper, or brass, require only a few seconds immersion, those of iron, or steel, a somewhat longer time. All articles should be well washed in clean water, immediately after taking them out of the potash solution, after which they should be treated with some of the different acid solutions, in order to more fully prepare the surface for the depositing solution. All articles of copper, brass, or German silver, should be dipped into a solution consisting of water four parts, sulphuric acid four parts, nitric acid two parts, to which a very small quantity of muriatic acid may be added. Articles of iron should be dipped in a mixture composed of one part of sulphuric acid and fifteen or twenty parts of water, and then well washed. Articles of lead, brittannia metal, or pewter, after having been treated with the potash solution and rinsed may be placed at once in the plating solution. It is a much better plan, however, to coat them, and articles of iron and steel also, with a thin film of copper by means of one of the following solutions before attempting to plate them with either gold, silver or nickel. For depositing a thin coating of copper on iron or steel use a weak and slightly acidulated solution of sulphate of copper, (blue vitriol) rub the articles briskly

with a cloth moistened with this liquid, and as
soon as they have the desired appearance, wash
them well and dry them quickly ; or they may
simply be immersed in the liquid for a short
time, and then thoroughly washed, and dried.
This solution is not adapted for any other metals
except iron and steel, and is not always certain·
in its operation.   The surest, and best way is to
use a battery and an alkaline solution, which may
be prepared in the following manner :   Add to
a solution of sulphate of copper, a solution of
cyanide of potassium just as long, but no longer
than it forms a precipitate ; the cyanide solution
should be added slowly, and towards the last in
small quantities at a time, with frequent stirring,
carefully observing when it no longer forms a
precipitate, which is cyanide of copper.   Allow
it to settle, and pour off the clear liquid,
wash the precipitate well by filling the vessel
with water, stirring it up, and after it has settled
again pouring off the water, repeating the
operation several times, in order to remove all
traces of acid, then add to the wet cyanide of
copper, a little more of a solution of cyanide of
potassium than is required simply to dissolve it,
that is, add the cyanide of potassium solution, to

the wet cyanide of copper, until it is all dissolved; then add a little more of the cyanide solution to form what is termed "free cyanide." This solution should be used at a temperature of about 150° Fahr. A battery of from one to three cells, such as are used in all telegraph offices, will be sufficient for all ordinary operations. To use this solution, immerse in it a clean sheet of copper and attach it to the wire leading from the copper pole of the battery, and the previously well cleaned articles of iron, steel, lead, brittannia metal, and in fact almost any metal to the wire leading from the zinc pole of the battery. The articles should be immersed in the solution before being connected to the battery, and the wire should be detached from them before taking them out of it. The amount of battery should be adjusted to the amount of surface presented by the articles to be plated. The smaller the articles, the less battery power will be required. A number of small articles may be attached to each other, or to the same wire, and be plated at one time. If too much battery be used, the copper will be deposited in the form of a dark metallic powder. This solution is rather difficult to manage, and is more expensive than a simple acidulated solution of sulphate of copper. This latter solution, however, cannot be used to plate iron, steel, lead, brittannia metal, etc., unless they have previously received a thin deposit of copper in the cyanide solution. The sulphate solution is used in precisely the same manner as the cyanide solution, and where heavy deposits are desired, it is much to be preferred. In coppering articles in this way, preparatory to plating them with another metal, a thin deposit will be sufficient, but as we have stated before, the sulphate solution will not answer, unless the articles have previously received a thin deposit of copper, and we must per force first use the cyanide solution, or in the case of iron and steel resort to the rather uncertain method of rubbing them with a rag, moistened with a slightly acidulated solution of the sulphate. After removing the articles from the solution, they should be well washed and examined, and if any imperfections be discovered, the cleaning and scouring operation will have to be done over again, and the plating repeated, but by using a proper amount of care the first attempt will generally prove successful.

NICKEL PLATING WITHOUT A BATTERY.

The commonest salts of nickel are the nitrate, chloride, sulphate and oxide. The nitrate is obtained by dissolving the metal in warm diluted nitric acid, and evaporating the mixture by a gentle heat until the residue solidifies upon cooling. The oxide is made by adding to a solution of the nitrate, or other common salt of nickel, a solution of potash or caustic soda, until it no longer forms a precipitate. There is no danger of adding too much of either potash or soda, as the oxide it forms is not soluble in a solution of either of them; the precipitate which is oxide of nickel, should be collected by means of a filter and dried. It is a black powder, insoluble in water, but dissolves readily in nitric, muriatic or sulphuric acid. The sulphate is obtained by dissolving either the nitrate, chloride or oxide in a quantity of diluted sulphuric acid, and evaporating the mixture nearly to dryness, when it will solidify upon cooling. A solution of the nitrate of nickel may be obtained by passing a tolerably strong current of electricity through a very dilute solution of nitric acid, by means of two plates of nickel, or by using a dilute solution of muriatic acid, the chloride may be obtained, and with a dilute solution of sulphuric acid, a solution of the sulphate is produced. Nickel is too highly electro positive a metal to be readily deposited upon other metals, unless they are more electro positive than itself. This constitutes one of the greatest difficulties in the way of successful nickel plating, but one which we think may be overcome by a careful observance of the directions given.

Thoroughly cleaned articles of copper, brass, and German silver, and articles of iron, steel, pewter, type metal etc., that have previously received a deposit of copper by the battery process, may be coated with nickel very readily in the following solution: Add to a boiling solution of pure tin tarter, a small quantity of nickel oxide heated to redness, which will impart a greenish tint to the liquid. Use the solution hot, and stir the articles about in it with a brass rod until they have acquired a good deposit, then take them out, wash and dry them, and if necessary, polish them with finely powdered chalk   This solution should yield a very brilliant deposit and is comparatively easy to manage, but the immersion of the least particle of zinc or iron in it will greatly impair its action. and perhaps ruin it.

ELECTRO NICKEL PLATING.

There are quite a number of solutions used by different platers, for depositing nickel by means of the electric current, any of which are capable of doing excellent work, but in the hands of an inexperienced person, they all prove rather difficult to manage. The simplest, and perhaps the best solution, is made by adding slowly to a solution of nitrate, or chloride of nickel, a solution of cyanide of potassium as long as a precipitate, or cloud is formed, pour off the clear liquid. Wash the precipitate, and dissolve it in a strong solution of cyanide of potassium, adding a very little more of the cyanide solution, than is required simply to dissolve it.

Another, and a very good solution for electro-nickel plating, is simply solution of chloride of nickel, and yields a very white and brilliant deposit. Still another solution is composed of sulphate of nickel two parts, tartaric acid (dissolved in water) one part, and potash (concentrated lye) one-tenth part, or the tartaric acid and potash may be a very little in excess of the figures given without injuring the solution. This solution we think is capable of giving better results than either of the others, and is much more simple in its preparation. There are quite a number of other solutions used to a greater or less extent by different electro-platers, but their preparation and maintenance involve difficult and complex operations that necessitate a thorough knowledge of chemistry and for that reason would be out of place here.

MANAGEMENT OF NICKEL PLATING SO-
LUTIONS.

Nickel plating solutions are more difficult to manage than those of either copper, silver or gold. The amount of nickel salts held in the solution may vary considerably without materially affecting its working. From three to eight ounces of the combined salts per gal on of water makes a very good working solution. When it contains less than this amount the working of the solution is retarded by the in-creased resistence it offers to the passage of the electric current, and when it contains more than the proper amount, the chemical action is im-peded by the solution being too nearly satu-rated. Electro plating is the product of electro chemical action, this phenomenon being called electro chemical action from the fact that a cur-rent of electricity passing through a suitable liquid produces a chemical change in it. Elec-tricity being the cause and chemical action the

result, hence the importance of having a solution that is a good conductor of electricity and
at the same time one that is capable of sustain-
ing the proper amount of chemical action necessary for its successful operation. Nickel being
a very brittle metal, it is rather difficult to obtain
suitable anodes. They are generally composed
of plates of cast nickel, and should present a
surface considerably larger than that of the
articles to be plated. Where anodes of cast
nickel cannot be obtained small fragments of
nickel may be suspended in the solution by
means of a frame work of platinum wire.

Nickel is a metal that is seldom obtained in
its pure state. It generally containing traces of
copper, carbon and other impurities which, dissolving with the anode, are either deposited or
fall to the bottom and form a black sediment.
It is a difficult matter to obtain a heavy deposit
of nickel, owing to its tendency to crack and
scale off, but for ordinary work there is no par-
ticular necessity in having a thick deposit, as it
is so extremely hard that a very thin coating
will, with ordinary usage, last for years where a
deposit of silver equally as thick would scarcely
last as many months. Nickel is not affected to

any great extent by exposure to the air or coal smoke, and in this respect it possesses an advantage over silver which is easily tarnished by exposure to sulphuretted gases. Nickel is very easily corroded by acids and forms very poisonous compounds, and for this reason should never be used for plating the interior of vessels used in cooking ; but for plating such articles as cream pitchers, sugar bowls, drinking cups, etc., it possesses the great advantage of being capable of retaining its polish and resisting rough usage for a long time.

From one to three cells of battery will generally be sufficient ; too much battery causing the metal to be deposited in the form of a black powder. The anode, either in the form of a plate of nickel, or composed of fragments of nickel suspended in a platinum wire net work, should be attached to the wire leading from the copper pole of the battery, and the previously cleaned articles, after being placed in the solution, should be attached to the wire leading from the zinc pole of the battery and kept in gentle but constant motion and as near as possible to the anode without coming in actual contact with it, until they have acquired a sufficient

3

deposit, when they may be taken out and well rinsed in hot water and dried by rolling them about in hot sawdust. All the solutions we have given should be used at a temperature of from 100° to 150° Fahr.

SILVER PLATING WITHOUT A BATTERY.

Quite a number of the different salts of silver have been used in forming preparations for silver plating by this method, which, by the way, hardly merits the name of silver plating, as but a very thin film of metal can be deposited without the aid of a battery, but for small articles of ornament not subject to much hard usage this process of silvering answers very well. Most of the salts of silver are made from the nitrate, which is formed by dissolving small fragments of silver in a warm mixture composed of one part of water and four or five parts of the strongest nitric acid. Care must be taken that the liquid is not too hot nor the silver added too rapidly, or it will boil over and a portion of it be lost. Should it threaten to do so, add a small quantity of cold water. The whole operation should be conducted in the open air or where there is sufficient draft to carry off the noxious fumes that arise from the mixture while the silver is being dissolved. When it will dissolve no more metal it should be evaporated and crystallized. The resultant salt is nitrate of silver, which should be kept in a well stoppered bottle protected from the light. The chloride is formed by adding a solution of common salt to a solution of nitrate of silver, until it will no longer form a precipitate, which should be carefully filtered and washed and be protected from the light. This salt is more frequently used in making compounds for silvering without a battery, than any of the other salts.

This process is more particularly adapted to the plating of small articles, where they are not subject to much wear, and consequently only a very thin coating of silver is required; the deposit looking fully as well as articles plated by the battery process.

The following solutions we have selected from a large number as being the most economical ; and at the same time, simple and efficacious, and are used by adding sufficient warm water to them to form a thin paste, and rubbing it over the articles with a soft rag, or stirring them about in it until they have become thoroughly coated.   1st. Take equal parts of chloride of silver and cream of tarter. 2d. Take common salt and cream of tarter each six parts, chloride of silver one part and about two parts of alum. A good liquid solution is made by dissolving in boiling water a mixture composed of chloride of silver one part and cream of tarter sixty or eighty parts. The articles to be plated should be placed in a small basket and immersed and stirred around in the boiling liquid.

The above mentioned solutions can only be used for plating articles of brass, copper or German silver, or articles of other metals that have previously received a coating of copper. The liquid solution, after continued use, becomes of a greenish color, caused by the presence of copper, dissolved from articles that have been plated in it. The presence of the least particle of iron, steel, lead or brittannia metal, causes the copper to be deposited, thus spoiling the appearance of the articles. An old solution, however, will work much better than a new one, provided it has been well taken care of and has been properly managed, and it may be renewed by occasionally adding small quantities of chloride of silver, and thus kept in good order for a

long time.   In using these solutions, as well as
all other plating solutions, the articles to be
plated must first be made very clean and smooth,
and the solutions kept at a uniform temperature.

SILVER PLATING BY THE BATTERY PROCESS.

Quite a number of the salts of silver have been used in forming solutions for silver plating by means of the electric current, all of which have proved more or less successful, but the solution that has the best stood the test of time and experience, is the commonly called cyanide solution, and which may be formed either by chemical means, or by means of an electric current. The former method, we think, is to be preferred, especially when the operation is to be conducted by those having but little experience in such matters. To prepare the solution by this method, make a solution of nitrate of silver in the proportion of about one pint of water to each half ounce of nitrate of silver; also have prepared a solution of cyanide of potassium in the proportion of about two ounces of cyanide of potassium to one quart of water, which should be added to the solution of nitrate of silver as long as any precipitate is formed (which is the cyanide of silver.) Should too much be added some of this precipitate will be redis solved and wasted. This will be indicated by a clear and slightly discolored tint being imparted to the liquid, where the cyanide of potassium solution passes. Should this be the case, add a weak solution of nitrate of silver in small quan· tities at a time, and at the same time stirring the liquid gently as long as it produces a light cloudy appearance. This amount of care is necessary in order that all of the silver may be utilized, as when too much or too little of the cyanide solution is added, some of the silver remains held in the solution. In the former case, in the shape of the double cyanide of silver and potassium, and when too little is added the silver remains in the clear portion of the solution in the form of nitrate of silver, but when just the proper amount is added, all of the silver is precipitated in the form of the simple cyanide of silver. After the exact neutral paint has been attained, allow the liquid to settle, and pour off the clear liquid, carefully preserving the precipitate which should be well washed by adding a quantity of water, stirring it up thoroughly, and after it has settled pour off the clear liquid, repeating the operation several times until all traces of acid have been removed. The wash waters, as well as the clear liquid first poured off should be preserved and tested in order to recover any traces of silver they may contain. Next add to the wet precipitate a strong solution of cyanide of potassium until barely the whole of it is dissolved, leaving a clear and light amber colored liquid. The cyanide solution should be added in small quantities at a time, and the solution thoroughly stirred upon each addition, then allow it to settle. Should any of the precipitate then remain undissolved, add a little more of the cyanide solution, stir briskly, and allow it to settle, repeating the operation until barely the whole is dissolved, and finally having observed how much of the cyanide of potassium solution was required to merely dissolve the precipitate, add about one-third to one half as much more of it, in order to form what is called "free cyanide," and then add enough water to dilute the whole to the proportion of about two ounces of nitrate of silver per gallon or more of the solution. The solution is then ready for immediate use.

There are also quite a number of methods other than this of making the cyanide solution, but all of them necessitate the introduction of various impurities that are often highly detrimental ; for instance, suppose we add a solution of cyanide of potassium to a solution of oxide of silver as long as it will dissolve, and then add the usual amount of free cyanide part of the cyanide of potassium will be converted into caustic potash, or if chloride of silver be used instead of th᛫ oxide, part of the cyanide of potassium will be converted into chloride of potash, or if the nitrate of silver be used, it will produce almost an equal amount of the nitrate of potash as an impurity in the solution. Nor is this process an economical one by any means, as it requires exactly the same amount of cyanide of potassium to convert it into the plating solution as where the solution is made by the method we have first given, and besides it has the very great disadvantage of introducing impurities very detrimental to the satisfactory working of the solution.

The strength of silver plating solutions may vary greatly without materially affecting their operation, some platers doing excellent work with solutions containing half an ounce of silver per gallon, and others using solutions containing several ounces of silver, and almost as many pounds of cyanide of potassium. A good working solution should contain from one to three ounces of silver per gallon, converted into cyanide, and from thirty to fifty per cent. of free cyanide. A good solution should not have a corroding effect on the base metals because it is those metals we wish to plate, and if the solution should have a corroding effect upon them, it will infallibly cause the deposit to strip and scale off. The cyanide silver plating solu· tion may be made by the battery process, with but very little trouble, and some electro platers prefer this method to any other, but while it possesses the advantage of simplicity, it also has the disadvantage of forming a small quan· tity of potash in the solution. This, however, may be remedied by the addition of a small quantity of the strongest prussic acid, which converts the caustic potash into cyanide. To make the solution by this process, make a moderately strong solution of cyanide of potas- sium and suspend in it a large anode and a small cathode of silver and then pass a strong current of electricity through it until a clean sheet of copper substituted for a short time for the small silver cathode, receives a good deposit of silver, or until the solution contains about one ounce of silver per gallon which may be determined by weighing both the anode and the cathode before placing them in the solution and then weighing them from time to time, until the proper amount of silver is known to have been dissolved, the solution is then ready for use.

The silver deposited by these solutions has a frosted appearance, and must be burnished in order to make them bright, or they may be placed in a specially prepared solution in order to deposit a coating of bright silver upon them.

This brightening solution is prepared by taking one pint of the ordinary silver plating solution, containing about two pounds of cyanide of potassium per gallon, and add to it two ounces of bisulphide of carbon, two of strong liquor ammonia and one of ether, and shake well. Let it stand at least twenty-four hours, shaking it occasionally, and then add the clear liquid to the ordinary silver plating solution, with gentle stirring in the proportion of one ounce to every ten gallons. This would make less than a small teaspoonfull per gallon. This brightening mixture should be added in the above proportions about every other day, but great care must be observed that too much is not used, as more solutions have been ruined by the excess of the brightening solution, than by all other causes put together. It is best to add but very little at first, and if from the working of the solution, you conclude it needs more, then add a very little more taking care to use only the very least possible amount necessary to produce the desired effect. If too much is added, it will cause the articles to have a dull and dark appearance, and perhaps to have dark streaks or spots on them. As often as a quantity of the brightening liquid is used, add a similar amount of the ordinary plating solution, or the same amount of a solution of cyanide of potassium, containing two pounds of cyanide of potassium per gallon. Another brightening solution is prepared by taking one quart of ordinary silver plating liquid containing about a half pound of cyanide of potassium, and adding to it two ounces of bisulphide of carbon, shaking well, and then set aside for a day or two, and adding to the ordinary plating solution in the same proportion as the first liquid we mention, always replacing the amount used by a similar amount of the ordinary silver plating solution, and shaking well. The "bright" solution is only used to finish articles in they having previously received a deposit in the ordinary plating solution, and then transferred immediately to the "bright" solution. Now having described the different methods of making the solutions, we will give the reader a few practical hints as to their management.

Copper, brass, and German silver become coated with silver much easier than any other metal, and for this reason all articles of other metals should, if possible, first receive a deposit of copper before attempting to plate them with silver. This, however, is not absolutely necessary, when plating by means of the electric current. All articles must of course be made perfectly clean before attempting to plate them and when the cleaning operation has been concluded, great care must be taken to prevent them coming in contact with anything that would tarnish them in the least, handling them only with metallic hooks or tongs and *never* with the naked hand.

Articles of iron and steel are first immersed in a hot and strong potash solution, then dipped for a short time only in a liquid prepared as follows: Take one pint of water, add to it slowly two ounces of sulphuric acid that has had a small piece of zinc dissolved in it and then add one ounce of nitric acid ; This should give the articles a clean bright appearance.

They may then be plated with copper in a cyanide solution as previously described or they may be placed in the ordinary silver plating solution, using a strong battery of considerable "quantity" at first, or until they have acquired a thin deposit, when the battery should be reduced to the ordinary strength, until the deposit is sufficiently heavy.

All articles should be suspended in the solution by means of a wire or hook of the same or similar metal, small articles may be strung on a wire of the same metal as the contact of different metals in the solution is apt to leave a stain.

Articles of copper, brass and German silver, after being thoroughly cleaned by means of the potash and acid solutions, should be immersed in the following solution and then well rinsed in clean water just previous to placing them in the silver solution: Dissolve one ounce of mercury in a mixture composed of nitric acid one part and water three parts, add no more mercury than the acid will dissolve, dilute it with as much more water and add a strong solution of cyanide of potassium as long as it forms a precipitate but no longer. Collect the precipitate and wash it two or three times with clear water, then add to it with occasional stirring a strong solution of cyanide of potassium until it is all dissolved, then add a little more of the cyanide solution and enough water to make the whole measure a gallon. This solution will cover the articles with a thin coating of mercury and will generally insure a firm adherent deposit.

The articles should not remain in the murcuric solution any longer than is necessary to make them look white, and should be well rinsed in water after taking them out, in order to remove all excess of it.

The solution will last a long time, but it finally becomes weak and impure from continued use, and blackens the articles immersed in it. It is then better to make a new solution than to try to revive the old one, almost any salt of mercury may be dissolved in a solution of cyanide of potassium to be used as a "quicking" solution. For instance, dissolve a quantity of red precipitate in an excess of a solution of cyanide of potassium ; that is, add the red precipitate as long as the cyanide solution will dissolve it; then add a small quantity of the cyanide solution.

The mercuric solution may be prepared in a number of ways, but the result is practically the same, viz. : The forming of a solution of the double cyanide of mercury and potassium.

The brightening solution works slower and requires a stronger battery than the ordinary solution ; it generally requiring from ten to twenty minutes for the articles to become wholly bright. The deposit is also much harder.

When the articles are once placed in the solution they must not be moved or disturbed until the operation is completed, and where a number of articles are being brightened at the same time none of them must be taken out or disturbed in any way until all of them have become bright.

When the articles have become sufficiently bright disconnect them from the battery and remove them from the solution and place them immediately in boiling water and allow them to remain there a few minutes, then take them out and dry them.

GOLD PLATING WITHOUT A BATTERY.

Chloride of gold is the salt generally used in making gilding solutions and in preparing the other salts of gold. The chloride of gold is prepared by dissolving gold in a warm aqua-regia which is a mixture composed of one part of nitric acid and two or three of muriatic acid. The gold should be cut up in small pieces and added slowly, care being taken not to inhale the gases that arise from the mixture. The gold dissolves very slowly but by gently heating the mixture its action is quickened. Four ounces of this liquid will dissolve about one ounce of gold, and form nearly one and a third ounces of chloride of gold.

When the solution has dissolved all the gold it can, evaporate it with gentle heat to a small bulk which will solidify when cooled. The resultant yellow salt is the chloride of gold which is soluble in water.

Almost all articles of gold contain traces of silver and this metal may now be observed in the solution in the form of chloride of silver, which is a white substance and insoluble in water, which may be removed, if desired, by pouring off the clear liquid, which holds the gold in solution, leaving behind the white chloride of silver, which should be preserved.

Any dark or brownish substance that will not dissolve is very likely metallic gold formed by the chloride being over heated and should be re·converted into chloride.

A solution of gold forms upon the addition of ammonia, a brown precipitate which, when dry, is one of the most powerful and dangerous ex plosives known, and which detonates with the least friction or percussion. One little accident of this kind will put a sudden stop to any further experiments, therefore great care should be taken to prevent its formation, or if formed to prevent its becoming dry.

The gilding solution is prepared as follows: Dissolve one pennyweight of chloride of gold in a gallon and a half of water; add nine ounces of caustic potash, one ounce of carbonate of potash, and half an ounce of cyanide of potash. This solution should be used very hot, but not quite at the boiling point.

The previously cleaned articles of copper or brass are immersed for a short time in this solution, when they should be taken out and dried. Should a thicker coating be desired they should then be dipped in the cyanide of mercury solution (see page 40) and then after rinsing them, be immersed in the gilding solu-tion again. By repeating this operation several times a very thick deposit may be obtained capable of resisting the action of the strongest acids for a long time.

This process of gold plating is more particu-larly adapted to the plating of articles not sub-ject to much handling, as generally only a very thin coating is obtained by it. The work done by this method, however, looks fully as well as that done by the battery process, and to those having no knowledge of the art of electro-metallurgy is somewhat more simple.

The solution also improves with constant usage, acquiring a greenish tint from the pres-ence of copper dissolved from the articles that have been plated in it. This however, does not interfere with its working unless there is a great deal of it held in solution , then it may be deposited with the gold, and impart a darker color to it.

As the solution gradually loses its gold by being deposited, it is necessary to add, from time to time, a small quantity of chloride of gold dissolved in a little water, in order to strengthen it, and after three or four such additions it may be necessary to add a small amount of the other salts, always preserving the proper proportions. By this means the solution may be kept in good working order for an indefinite length of time.

GOLD PLATING BY THE BATTERY PROCESS.

Solutions for gold plating by means of the electric current may, like those for silver plating be made either by the aid of a battery, or by the chemical process; that made by the chemical process being more quickly made and we think capable of giving better satisfaction to the inexperienced.

The solution made by the battery process has the advantage of being perhaps a trifle more economical, and for this reason is often preferred by the experienced electro plater.

To make the solution by the chemical process, dissolve about one and a half ounces of chloride of gold in water or convert a little over an ounce of gold into chloride and dissolve in water. and add a solution of cyanide of potassium, slowly and at intervals with frequent stirring just as long as it produces a precipitate, but no longer. Great care must be taken to attain the exact neutral paint, that is, when it no longer produces a precipitate upon the addition of a very small quantity of either the cyanide or the chloride of gold solution.

A small quantity of the chloride of gold solution should be reserved and slightly diluted for this purpose, and if it is not all used it may be set away and protected from the light for future use.

Should the solution contain an excess of either the chloride or the cyanide some of the gold will be held in the clear solution and be poured off, hence the importance of exercising great care in this respect.

When the exact neutral paint has been attained, allow it to settle and pour off the clear liquid, which should be preserved in order to recover any traces of gold it may contain. Then wash the precipitate well by adding water, stirring briskly, and after it has settled, pouring off the clear liquid, repeating the operation a number of times so as. to thoroughly remove all traces of acid.

The wash waters should be preserved as they also are liable to contain traces of gold.

After the last wash water has been poured off pour the precipitate into a paper filter, add a small quantity of water and allow it to drain thoroughly, but not to become dry, as it may possibly contain a small amount of the fulminate of gold which is an extremely dangerous substance, and detonates with terrible violence upon the slightest friction or percussion. When the precipitate has thoroughly drained, collect it in a suitable vessel and add to it a strong solution of cyanide of potassium until barely the whole of it is dissolved, then, having observed the amount of cyanide solution neces sary to merely dissolve the precipitate, add about one-fourth as much more to form what is termed by electro platers "free cyanide" and finally dilute the whole with clean water to one gallon. The amount of gold in the solution may vary greatly from the amount we have given without injury to its working, but in order to obtain the best results it should not contain less than one half an ounce, nor more than ten ounces of gold per gallon. A rather dilute solution gives a somewhat better deposit but is less rapid in its operation than a stronger one.

To prepare the gilding solution by means of a battery, dissolve two pounds of cyanide of potassium in one gallon of warm water, immerse two sheets of pure gold in this solution and connect them to a moderately strong battery, and allow them to remain in this position and occasionally stirring the liquid, until the proper amount of gold has been dissolved and held in solution. This may be determined by weighing both sheets of gold before placing them in the solution, and then by taking them out of the solution occasionally and weighing them, the amount of gold held in solution may be very easily determined.

Still another and a better means of ascertaining when the solution is ready for use, is to occasionally substitute for a short time a bright and clean sheet of copper, or light colored brass for the gold cathode, until it finally receives a satisfactory deposit. The solution is then ready for work and should be used at a temperature of about 150° Fahr.

PRACTICAL OPERATION OF GILDING SO-LUTIONS.

All solutions for gold plating should be used at a temperature of about 150° Fahr., and when not in use should be carefully covered over to protect it from the dust and other impurities. The amount of gold held in the solution may vary greatly without materially affecting it working, provided always, that it also contains a proportionate amount of cyanide of potassium. The proportions of gold and cyanide of potassium in the solution may vary within certain limits, generally from twenty-five to fifty per cent. more than is required to simply dissolve the cyanide of gold (see page 49) without impairing its usefulness.

Too much cyanide of potassium causes the deposit to have a dirty discolored appearance. After the solution has been in use for some time it often works badly in consequence of the proportions of gold and cyanide becoming disarranged. This is caused sometimes by using anodes with greater or less surface than the articles to be plated.

When the anode presents a larger surface in the solution than the articles to be plated, the solution rapidly becomes richer in gold, which uniting with the free cyanide, soon uses it all up in forming the double cyanide of gold and potassium, leaving but very little or none at all to form the "free cyanide" so essential to its perfect working.

This condition is indicated by the anode becoming covered with crust or sediment, and is remedied by using an anode with smaller surface than the articles to be plated, or a sufficient amount of a solution of cyanide of potassium may be added.

When the anode becomes black, and has a slimy appearance, the solution needs more gold, which may be supplied by using an anode of greater surface until the solution is again properly proportioned, which will be indicated by the anode remaining bright and clean and giving a good deposit. By carefully observing these indications, and applying the proper remedy, the solution may be kept in order almost indefinitely, but after very long continued use it becomes contaminated with various impurities, some of them accidentally introduced, and others set free by the dissolving of the anode.

Gold anodes invariably contain traces of silver, which is dissolved in the solution, and by being deposited with the gold increases its paleness of color. When from any of these reasons the solution ceases to work satisfactorily, all the metal held in solution may be recovered separately, and used to start out anew.

DEPOSITING DIFFERENT SHADES OF GOLD.

The color of the deposit may be regulated in quite a number of ways, pure gold having too light a color to be admired by many. An old solution, in which a great many copper articles have been plated, is capable of yielding different colored deposits by means of regulating the size of the anodes, temperature of the solution, the strength of the battery, and, in a degree, the strength of the solution also.

An old solution, that yields a pale yellow deposit, when but a small portion of the anode touches the solution, will yield a darker deposit when the anode is further immersed, and finally, when it is entirely immersed, the deposit will be of a red color.

The temperature of the solution effects the color of the deposit, it being much darker and richer when the solution is used hot than when it is used cold, and it is claimed by a great many electro-platers, and justly too, that a metal deposited from a warm solution is harder, and consequently more durable, than a metal deposited from a cold solution.

The strength of the battery also has a great deal to do with the color of the deposit, a moderately weak current producing a much lighter colored deposit than that produced by a much stronger battery. There are, however, certain limits regulating both the temperature and battery power, beyond which it is not safe to venture. The temperature should never be allowed to greatly exceed 160° Fahr.

The amount of battery power is a more difficult matter to determine, as it varies with the amount of surface presented by the articles to be plated. Generally speaking, three cups of the ordinary Callaud or gravity battery will be amply sufficient for operations on the larger scale, while one, or, perhaps, two cups will answer for the gilding of small articles, or electro-plating on a small scale.

Gold deposited by the electric current is not always pure gold, as other metals are often deposited with it in order to produce the desired color or tint, and in large electro plating establishments, or where a great variety of work is done, a number of gilding solutions are used, each of them yielding a different colored deposit. However, one solution is capable of yielding, with careful and judicious management, a deposit of gold varying in color from the light yellow of almost pure gold, to a deposit so alloyed with copper as to resemble 14 karat gold, and which it really is.

In order to accomplish this, the solution must contain a small amount of copper. This metal is always present in old gilding solutions, caused by a very minute portion of the metal being dissolved from each article of copper that has been plated in the solution. Of course the amount of metal dissolved from each individual article is very small indeed, but when in the course of time a great many of them have been plated, the aggregate of the dissolved copper is considerable, and quite sufficient to change the color of the deposit. A freshly made solution used quite hot, with a large gold anode and a tolerably strong battery, will generally give a satisfactory deposit, but should it still be of too light a color, remove the gold anode and substitute in its place a clean one of copper and work the solution with it until the deposit begins to slightly change its color, and then replace it with the gold anode. If the copper anode has been weighed before, and again just after using it, as above mentioned, it will be discovered that a portion of it has been dissolved in the solution, which by being deposited with the gold gives it a richer and darker color.

To obtain a green colored deposit, add a small quantity of the ordinary silver plating solution to the gilding solution, with gentle stirring, taking care to add just enough to produce the desired effect, as where too much of the silver solution is added it is liable to spoil it.

White gilding is produced by adding a solution of nitrate of silver to the gilding solution, until the desired colored deposit is obtained, which must be ascertained by actual trial.

Pink gold is obtained by first plating the articles in a cold and weak solution, with a weak battery, then giving them another coat in a hot and strong solution that has considerable copper in it, using a more powerful battery in order to obtain a dark colored deposit, then give them an exceedingly thin coating in the ordinary silver plating solution, and finally burnish them. The coating of silver should be barely sufficient to impart a lighter tinge to the deposit which, if the operation has been successful, will be of a beautiful pink color when burnished.

To gild the inside surface of articles, such as cups, cream pitchers, and similar articles, fill them with the solution, and suspend a gold anode in them, and attach the article itself to the wire leading from the zinc pole of the battery. The lips of the pitcher, and other portions that the solution does not touch, may be plated by laying a rag wetted with the gilding solution upon the part, leaving a portion of it immersed in the solution contained in the vessel. The outside surface of the article, or that portion of it you may not want to gold plate, may be coated with a solution of sealing wax dissolved in naptha, or simply painted over with melted beeswax, and the articles placed in the gilding solution in the ordinary way, and after the gilding operation has been completed, the wax is easily removed.

REPLATING OLD ARTICLES.

In order to obtain a good satisfactory deposit upon old articles, the old plating must first be entirely removed, or they will be apt to show lines, where the old and the new plating join.

The removing of the old deposit may be accomplished, by making them the *anode* in a solution composed of one pound of cyanide of potassium in one gallon of water, using a sheet of copper for the cathode. This process is always used for articles of iron, steel, lead, brittania metal, and pewter and sometimes for articles of copper, brass and German silver. Articles made of the latter metals are generally "stripped" of their old deposit in an acid solution, which is made by adding a small quantity of saltpetre (nitrate of soda) to a quantity of hot and strong sulphuric acid sufficient to cover the articles. Should action become slow, it may be quickened by adding more saltpetre, and using the solution at a higher temperture.

After the old plating has been removed, they should be well washed in clean water, scratch brushed, and treated with the various acid and mercuric solutions as described on page 39, in order to prepare the surface for the gilding solution. The "stripping" solution will not act upon the copper or brass base of the articles to any very great extent, unless they are allowed to remain in it too long.

The articles should be perfectly dried before immersing them, in order to keep the solution as free from water as possible.

This solution is probably the best for operations on a small scale, as the amount, or bulk of it, need not be much more than barely sufficient to cover the articles.

Another solution is prepared by adding ten parts of strong sulphuric acid to one of nitric acid. A large quantity of this solution is required, which should be kept as free from water as possible by taking care that the articles to be "stripped" are first thoroughly dried, and by keeping the vessel containing it closely covered to prevent its aborbing moisture from the air. This solution should be used cold, and as it becomes weaker, add very small quantities of nitric acid to it.   The addition of a small quantity of water will cause it to attack the copper base of the articles.

In stripping old articles to be replated, care must be taken to remove every traces of the old d posit, in order that the new one may present a clean, smooth and evenly colored appearance.

Some platers, however, replate old articles without first removing the old plating, by washing and scouring them well, then brushing them thoroughly with a wire scratch brush, (see page 72), and finally, after treating them with the acid and mercuric solution, (see page 40), placing them at once in a tolerable strong silver solution, and using a battery of considerable strength at first, diminishing the battery power as the plating operation progresses.

This plan is not an economical one, as the deposit is doubled upon that portion of the articles subject to the least wear, and giving the other portions a much lighter coat, where they need it the most.   This process also requires that a thicker plating be deposited, in order to cover up the lines that are liable to occur where the old and the new deposits join, and which by the way, is an extremely difficult matter to do, as scratches and lines have a tendency to magnify themselves during the plating process, and where a very thick deposit is obtained, a slight scratch often becomes a crack of consid crable size.

About the only remedy for this is to take them out of the plating solution quite often and brush them well, and while in the solution they should be kept in gentle but constant motion.

In re-gilding old articles, the old deposit should first be removed by making them the anode in a warm solution composed of one pound of cyanide of potassium in one gallon of water, using a battery of considerable strength until all of the old plating has all been dissolved. They should then be well washed and brushed in clean water and prepared for the plating solution by treating them with the various acid and mercuric solutions described on pages 39 and 40.

HOW TO MAKE A BATTERY.

One of the best batteries for electro-plating purposes is the ordinary gravity battery, of which there are various styles, all of them, however, being made on the same general plan.

To construct a battery of this kind, procure two or three pieces of sheet copper five or six inches long, and about two inches wide and fasten them together by means of a copper rivet through the center; to the end of one of the strips fasten a copper wire about a foot long by means of another copper rivet. The wire must be well insulated except at its two extremities, in order to prevent its being corroded at the surface of the solution.

India rubber is the best substance for this purpose and is generally used in batteries of this description, but where wire already coated with rubber cannot be procured, a very good substitute may be obtained by wrapping the wire carefully with tarred twine and giving it a final coating of melted beeswax, containing a very little lard.

The zinc electrode is more difficult to make, and where it is convenient it will be more economical to buy them. They are made in a number of shapes, the object being to obtain an electrode exposing the largest amount of surface to the action of the solution for a given weight of metal, and a the same time to be of such a shape as to allow the bubbles of hydrogen gas formed by the action of the battery to escape freely.

A very convenient form is that of a wheel with six spokes, the "hub" projecting upward about two or two and a half inches with the connecting wire cast in the center of it. This wire should be from from from four to six inches in length.

Zincs of this kind are suspended in the solution by passing the wire through a hole in a small flat piece of wood long enough to reach across the vessel, and is fastened to it at the proper height by means of a small clamp of any kind, or by simply taking a turn of the connecting wire around the supporting stick. A very good clamp for securing the zincs in position may be made by drilling a hole large enough to admit the wire, throug a small piece or block of metal, and then drilling another hole at right angles, and intercepting the first one, and fitting it with a screw, and is used by slipping it over the connecting wire until it rests on the wooden support, and fastening it to the wire by means of the screw.

Zincs are often cast in the form of a thick ring with a hook shaped projection of the same metal extending upwards about three inches and at right angles with the ring. This zinc is used by attaching it to the jar by simply hooking it over the edge. The top of the "hook" has two holes drilled in it, intercepting each other, one of them being fitted with a set screw for clamping the connecting wire.

There are several other forms of zincs, but these two we have described embody the main features of all the others and of these two we think the first is the best on account of the larger amount of surface exposed and the more economical distribution of the metal.

The dimensions of a well proportioned zinc should be from five to six inches wide, one inch to one inch and a half high, and the spokes and rim about three-eighths to half an inch thick.

The jar for containing the battery should be about ten inches high and from six to seven inches wide, with straight sides and flat bottom, and may be of either glass or earthen ware.

To set the battery in operation, fill the jar with water to within two inches of the top and add one pound of sulphate of zinc. When it is all dissolved take the copper electrode and bend the strips outward until their ends are all about equally distant, and place it in the bottom of the jar ; then add a small handfull of sulphate of copper and suspend the zinc in the solution, about two inches above the copper, and in a short time the battery will be ready for use. When using more than one jar or cell of battery at one time they should be connected together by attaching the zinc of one jar to the copper of the next, the zinc of the second to the copper of the third, and so on, leaving the copper of the first and the zinc of the last jar for connecting with the wires leading from the plating solution.

When not in use the terminal wires should be connected together in order that the battery may continue to work, otherwise the blue solution will gradually raise, and in a few days time surround the zinc and soon destroy it. When the blue solution has almost disappeared add a few crystals of sulphate of copper. After being in use for some time the solution becomes saturated with sulphate of zinc, which will creep up the sides and over the top of the vessel and greatly impair its working. When this is observed draw off about a pint from the *top* of the solution, and replace it with water, taking care not to stir the solution.

This form of battery is termed the "gravity battery" because the two solutions which are employed in it, sulphate of zinc and sulphate of copper, are separated, but allowed to touch each other by taking advantage of the difference in their weights, the sulphate of copper solution being the heaviest, remaining at the bottom sur rounding the copper electrode, and the sulphate of zinc, being the lightest, remains at the top and surrounds the sinc.

After this battery has been in use five or six months the zincs will require renewing, the copper in the meantime having greatly increased in size, the copper of the sulphate of

copper havin been deposited upon it, while the
liberated sulphuric acid attacked the zinc, forming sulphate of zinc. When the deposit upon
the copper has become about a quarter of an
inch thick, it should be removed by bending the
strip until the deposit cracks. It may then be
easily removed by inserting a chisel between it
and the original copper strip. Quite a quantity
of perfectly pure copper may be collected in
this manner, which is valuable, and should be
preserved.

The zincs should be taken out at least once a
month, and thorougly scraped and cleaned.

This battery is preferred for electro-plating
operations on account of the steady, uniform
current it produces, which is a very important
consideration in obtaining a good deposit.

The strength of the current may be varied by
raising or lowering the zinc in the solution.
When a weak current is desired the zinc should
be raised so that but a very small portion of it
is immersed in the solution, the greatest strength
being obtained when all the zincs are wholly
immersed.

This battery possesses a very great advantage
over all others, from the fact that it always gen-

erates a current of uniform strength during long
continued action, which is something that other
batteries, although generating a more powerful
current, often fail to do. It is also much more
easily managed, and requires less care and atten-
tion to keep it in good working order, and, in
fact, the only objection that can be legitimately
raised against it is, that it deteriorates rapidly when
not in active service, the blue vitrol solution,
raising slowly, but surely, and finally surround-
ing the zinc, which is quickly corroded and
rendered unfit for use until it has been thoroughly cleaned. When there is but little work
to do, and the battery forced to remain idle the
greater part of the time, the old style "Daniel"
battery will probably give the best results. It
consists of a strip of copper five or six inches
wide and fifteen or eighteen inches long, rolled
in the form of a cylinder that will fit the inside
of the battery jar loosely. Inside of this copper
cylinder is placed an earthenware cup which, in
the abesnce of regular porous cups, made
especially for this style of battery, may consist
of a small unglazed flower pot, the hole in the
bottom being securely stopped up. Inside of

this porous cup is placed a bar, or better still, a small cylinder of zinc.

To put the battery in operation, fill the outer jar with a solution of blue vitrol, and the porous cup containing the zinc, with a tolerably strong solution of sulphate of zinc, or a mixture of ten or twelve parts of water, to which one part of sulphuric acid is added slowly, may be used instead. The blue vitrol solution must be kept strong, and completely saturated, by carefully observing that there is at all times a few crystals of blue vitrol in the solution, and by adding a small handfull, from time to time, as fast as it is dissolved. The zinc should be supported in some way, and not allowed to touch the sides, or bottom of the porous cup. This is usually accomplished by laying a small stick across the porous cup, and suspending the zinc from it by the connecting wire.

This battery generates a steady and uniform cnrrent, but of less strength than that generated by the "Gravity" battery. When the battery is to remain idle any considerable length of time, the zincs and coppers should be taken out, washed and laid away, and the porous cups removed and the liquid they contain poured into a bottle and preserved for future use. The blue vitrol solution may remain in the larger outside jar, which should be carefully covered over to keep out the dust.

NOTES.

In preparing articles to receive a deposit, and also during the plating process, the scratch brush plays a very important part. It is made by wrapping a bundle of fine and hard brass wires tightly with another wire, leaving a small portion of each end free to form a kind of a stiff brush. Where practicable there should be three or four such brushes of different degree of fineness and temper, or one end of the brush may be anealed so as to be softer than the other end.

It very often happens that the deposit is slightly "off color," or has a gritty, sandy appearance. When this is the case the articles should be removed from the plating solution and well brushed and returned for the deposit to be finished.

In the larger electro-plating establishments the "lathe brush" is used almost exclusively, and consists of a small wheel from which the wires radiate, and which is attached the axle of the lathe.

The "scratch brush" is not always absolutely necessary, and may be dispensed with when doing small jobs, but for plating on the larger scale it will be found a most valuable aid. Its uses are manifold.

In cleansing articles they should be well brushed immediately upon taking them out of the potash solution, and also upon taking them out of the acid solutions, should they have a dark or discolored appearance.

When a thick deposit of metal is desired they should be taken out of the plating solution and well brushed to secure a regular and even deposit.

Sometimes the articles while in the plating solution become dark colored and presents a dirty appearance. This is generally caused by the battery power being too great in proportion to the size of the articles. When this is ob served to be the case take them out, wash and brush them well, treat them again with the mercuric solution and try it again, this time, however, reducing the power of the electric current, by lessening the number of cells of the battery used, or else by raising all of the zincs partly out of the battery solution.

The difficuly may also be overcome by plating a greater number of articles at the same time, the power of the electric current being thereby distributed over a great amount of surface. The solution may work badly on account of its being improperly made, or the ingredients becoming disproportioned by constant use, or they may contain acids accidentally introduced that will corrode the articles.   In any case they must be taken out and well washed, and if the difficulty is in the solution it should be remedied before attempting to plate them again.

After the plating operation has been success· fully accomplished the articles should be well "scratch brushed," and then burnished, unless it is desired to make them bright in the bright· ening solution.

The burnisher is a very hard and smooth piece of steel, highly polished, and and fitted with a suitable handle.   The articles to be burnished, after being well scratch brushed, are moistened with sour beer and rubbed with the burnishing tool until they have become perfectly bright.

Whenever the shape or design of the article will admit of it, they should be secured in a suitable vice or clamp, the jaws or face of which have been covered with a thick piece of cloth to prevent any injury by scratching or crushing them. The burnisher should be grasped with both hands, one near each end, and drawn rather briskly backward and forward over the surface of the articles, using only sufficient force to produce the desired result.

The interior of hollow articles, such as pitchers, drinking cups, etc., and articles of intricate design, require burnishing tools of different shapes, adapted to the general outline of the surface to be made bright.

Electro-deposited nickel is a very difficult metal to burnish, owing to its extreme hardness. It is much better to deposit this metal in a bright state than to attempt to burnish it.

WATER.—The water used in all plating operations, both in mixing the various chemicals, and in making the plating solutions, should either be distilled or well filtered rain water; spring and well water invariably containing various impurities, very detrimental to the working of the solutions. It should form no cloud upon the addition of a few drops of nitrate of silver.

NITRIC ACID.—This acid is sometimes aqua fortis. Only the best and strongest acid should be used for dissolving silver to form the nitrate of silver. A small portion of it largely diluted with pure distilled water should form no cloud upon the addition of a drop of a strong solution of nitrate of silver. It should be kept in strong well stoppered bottles, in a dark, cool and dry place.

Care should be taken not to inhale any of the fumes that arise from the acid.

Should a drop of this or any other acid fall upon the clothes, apply freely and at once, a quantity of diluted aqua ammonia.

HYDROCHLORIC ACID.—This acid is best known as muriatic acid, and when pure should be almost colorless, and of a specific gravity not less than 120° This acid is formed by the chemical union, or combination of hydrogen and chlorine. Hence the name hydro chloric acid.

AQUA REGIA.—This acid is a mixture of nitric and hydro-chloric acids in the proportion of one volume of nitric and from one to three parts of hydro-chloric acids, the strongest and best results being obtained when the proportions are about one of nitric and two of hydrochloric acids. It should not be prepared until required for immediate use, as it deteriorates rapidly.

SULPHURIC ACID.—This acid is sometimes called "oil of vitriol," and when pure should be almost, or quite colorless, and should be kept in a strong bottle with a close fitting glass stopper, as the particles of dust, wood, cork, or other organic matter quickly imparts a dark, brownish color to it.

When diluting this acid it is highly important that the acid should be poured very slowly into the water, and never the reverse. Both the acid and water should also be quite cold, as great heat is evolved upon mixing them. *Should a quantity of hot water be suddenly added to an equal amount of sulphuric acid, a violent explosion is almost certain to take place.*

BISULPHIDE OF CARBON.—This is a very volatile and inflammable liquid, and for this reason should be carefully kept away from a lighted lamp, stove or other source of heat or flame.

CHLORIDE OF GOLD.—This salt is sometimes called "muriate of gold," and may be purchased in almost any drug store, or may be easily prepared by any chemist. The commercial salt is often very impure, and largely adulterated with other cheaper salts. It may be prepared in the following manner :

For each ounce of gold to be dissolved, prepare four ounces of aqua regia, using only the best and strongest acids. The mixture should be slightly warm, and the gold added slowly in small fragments, until it is all dissolved. Should the action become slow, it may be quickened by heating the mixture, and stirring with moderate heat until it has been evaporated to a small bulk which will solidify upon cooling, forming a yellow salt which should be readily dissolved in water. Should it contain a white powder that will not dissolve in water, it is chloride of silver, formed from traces of that metal being present in the gold.

FULMINATE OF GOLD.—This salt is a dark, brown powder, and *very highly explosive*. It is formed by the addition of ammonia, or a solution of any salt of ammonia to a solution of chloride of gold. It is sometimes used in forming electro-gilding solutions, but owing to its dangerous properties, the inexperienced operator should never undertake its manufacture.

NITRATE OF SILVER.—This salt is in the form of small clear crystals, and should be free from any odor of nitric acid, and be freely soluble in pure water.

It is formed by dissolving pure silver in warm and slightly diluted nitric acid (about one part of pure water to four parts of strong nitric acid.) The silver should be cut up in small pieces and added slowly. Should the action become too rapid, and the mixture threaten to boil over, add a small quantity of *cold* water ; but, if the silver is added very slowly, and the mixture not too warm in the first place, there will be no trouble of this kind. Should the action be too slow, it may be quickened by applying more heat.

When it will dissolve no more metal, evaporate the solution, with a gentle heat, to a small bulk, and, when cooled, it will crystalize.

This salt is the nitrate of silver, which should be carefully collected and placed in a bottle, and kept in a dark place, or the bottle may be wrapped in a black paper or cloth to prevent the light acting upon the nitrate of silver, which, by the way, is the salt used by the photogra-phers in coating their plates in order to make them sensitive to the action of the light.

CHLORIDE OF SILVER.—This salt is somtimes called muriate of silver, and is extensively used in forming solutions for plating articles without the aid of a battery. It is generally prepared by adding a strong solution of common table salt to a solution of nitrate of silver, until it will no longer form a precipitate. No harm will be done if an excess of the solution of salt be added, and it is best to add enough to make certain that all of the silver has been precipi-tated. A quantity of dilute muriatic acid may be used, in place of the solution of salt, and will give the same result.

When all the silver has been precipitated, pour off the clear liquid and carefully collect and wash the residue, which is chloride of sil-ver. It should be kept in a well corked bottle and carefully protected from the light until ready for use.

MERCURY.—This metal is better known as
"quicksilver," and, when pure, should look perfectly bright and clean. It should not be allowed
to accidentally touch any metal, except iron or
platinum, as with most of the other metals it
forms an amalgam. It also volatilizes entirely
by being heated.

This property of the metal is taken advantage
of in gold and silver mining. The ore is first
crushed and powdered into a fine powder, by
powerful machinery, and then mixed with the
mercury, in large pans ; all of the gold, silver,
copper and other metals unite with the mercury
and form an amalgam, and the powdered rock,
now robbed of its metal, is washed away to
make room for a fresh supply, which is treated
in the same way, until the mercury becomes so
saturated with other metals that it can no longer
be used. This is determined by occasionally
testing it with the fingers. When it retains an
impression or dent it is known to be fully
charged with other metals, and is ready to be
freed of them.

This is accomplished by molding the amalgam
in the form of small balls, with the hands, and
placing them in a retort, to the top of which a

pipe is connected, leading to a vessel containing
cold water. Upon applying heat, the mercury
volatilizes and goes through the pipe, in the
form of vapor, but condenses by the time it
reaches the water, where it is collected in the
form of perfectly pure mercury, and may then
be used over again.

SULPHATE OF COPPER.—This salt is also known
as "blue vitrol," or "blue stone," and should be
in the form of tolerably large crystals of a beautiful deep blue color. It sometimes contains
iron, which is indicated by crystals having a
greenish hue.

HYDROCYANIC ACID.—This acid is better
known as "prussic acid." It is a clear liquid,
and is composed of water charged with cynogen
gas. It is one of the most violent and deadly
poisons known in chemical or medical science.
It is very dangerous to leave the bottle containing it uncorked, as the vapor or gas arising from
it is extremely poisonous.

It should be kept in a dark bottle, and well
protected from the light.

CYANIDE OF POTTASSIUM.—This substance, also, is a deadly poison, and produced almost as fatal results when absorbed by the skin as when swallowed.

It is generally procured in small, irregular sized lumps, of a white or very light grey color. It should be kept in strong and well stoppered bottles, as it absorbs moisture rapidly when ex posed to the air.

The cyanide of potasssium procured from chemists or in drug stores, varies greatly in strength and purity, and for this reason it is often more desirable to manufacture the article than to purchase it.

It is most conveniently and nearly always made in the following manner : Take a quantity of prussiate of potash (ferrocyanide of potas sium), and grind it up well in a mortar or other-wise reduce it to a fine powder, and dry it, by a gentle heat, in an iron pan, with c nstant stir-ring. In the meantime have an iron vessel, large enough to contain double the amount of the powdered prussiate of potash, heated red hot. When the powdered prussiate of potash has become thoroughly dry, put a small quan-tity of it in the red hot iron vessel, and wait until it has all melted; then add a little more of it, and so on, until the whole of it is melted, the vessel being covered as much as possible with a close-fitting iron lid, as during the whole operation a great deal of poisonous gas is evolved from the mixture.

After it has all been melted, it should be kept in that condition for about ten, or, perhaps, fifteen minutes, or, until a sample is procured by dipping a small iron rod in the mixture, has a white color. It should then be allowed to stand quiet for a few minutes, in order to permit the impurities to settle to the bottom. This may be aided by gently tapping the sides of the vessel.

The clear liquid remaining at the top is the pure cyanide of potassium, which should be carefully poured off in a shallow iron jar, and allowed to cool. Before it has become quite cold it should be broken up into small lumps with a light hammer, taking care that none of the fragments get into the eyes or mouth.

The sediment at the bottom of the vessel, will contain a large quantity of cyanide of potassium, which may be obtained by dissolving it in water, and straining or filtering the solution through a heavy, and closely woven piece of white cotton goods or regular filtering paper ; it should, however, be scraped out of the vessel while still hot, as when cold it is quite a difficult matter to break it.

RECOVERING TRACES OF METAL FROM WASH WATERS.

In making the salts of gold and silver the liquid first poured off, as well as the subsequent wash waters should be preserved and tested for any traces of metal they may contain. In the preparation of the salts of gold, the wash waters should be made slightly acid by the addition of a small quantity of muriatic acid and number of clean sheets of zinc immersed in the solution, and allowed to remain for some time. This will cause all the gold to be precipitated. When the solution contains chloride of gold it may be precipitated by adding a solution of sulphate of iron ("green vitriol" or "copperas.")

There are a number of ways of recovering gold from old gilding solutions, but almost all of them are very complex and difficult operations for inexperienced persons to perform, and require a good knowledge of chemistry.

One method is to evaporate the solution to dryness, powder it and mix it with an equal

amount by weight of litharge, then place it in a
platinum crucible and melt it; the result will be
a small lump of gold, alloyed with other metals,
generally with lead. This is removed by placing
the lump in a vessel containing hot nitric acid.
This will leave the pure gold in a loose spongy
mass, which may be melted over again and cast
in the form of a bar.

Another method for recovering the metallic
gold from old solutions, is as follows :

Add muriatic acid to the plating solution
until it is strongly acid. This may be tested by
means of test papers, that may be procured in
almost any drug store. The addition of the
muriatic acid causes a disengagement of large
volumes of hydro–cyanic acid gas, which is
extremely poisonous, and for this reason
the operation should be conducted in the open
air, or where there is good ventilation. A
precipitate is formed also, which is the cyanide
of gold, cyanide of copper, and perhaps a small
quantity of the chloride of silver. This precipitate is carefully collected and washed by
adding water to it, stirring it briskly, and after
it has settled, pouring off the clear liquid,
repeating the operation several times, it is then

dried and dissolved in cold aqua regia [see page 76], which dissolves the gold and copper, and leaves the chloride of silver in the form of a white or light colored powder. This solution is then evaporated almost to dryness, and the resultant salt dissolved in water, and the gold precipitated from it in the form of a brownish metallic powder by the addition of a solution of sulphate of iron. The metallic silver may be separated from the chloride of silver by mixing it with a somewhat larger quantity of the dry carbonate of sodium, and melting the mass in a crucible. A small lump of pure silver is the result.

RECOVERING SILVER FROM OLD SILVER PLATING SOLUTIONS.

Add muriatic acid to the plating solution until it is strongly acid. This will cause the liberation of a large quantity of hydrocyanic acid gas, which, as we have stated before, is very poisonous, and should, under no circumstances, be inhaled. It also causes a precipitate of silver, in the form of chloride of silver, which should be a very light or pure white color, but is more often tinted with red, owing to the copper nearly always present in old solutions, being precipitated with the silver. The The copper can be removed, if desired, after the precipitate has been washed by treating it with warm muriatic acid. This dissolves the copper and leaves the chloride of silver unchanged, which may be converted into metallic silver, by the process described on page 88, or, it may be used in forming a new plating solution.

7

In making nitrate of silver the liquid first poured off, as well as all the wash waters should be preserved, mixed together, and a strong solution of common salt or dilute muriatic acid added to them until it ceases to produce a precipitate.

This precipitate is the chloride of silver, which should be well washed, and may then be converted into metallic silver, or placed in a well stoppered bottle, and laid away for future use, as occasion may require, but it must be care fully protected from the light, which decomposes it rapidly.

The recovery of metal from the stripping liquids, may be accomplished by evaporating them down to a very small bulk, which will crystalize upon cooling. The residue is then dissolved in water, and the metal precipitated by means of strong solution of common salt, or by dilute muriatic acid.

The precipitate thus formed will likely contain a small amount of copper, which is dissolved by warm muriatic acid, and leaves the pure chloride of silver.

APPENDIX.

PYRO PLATING.—During the last few years a new process of causing a deposit of gold, silver, nickel and copper to adhere more firmly to such metals as iron and steel and other metals that do not readily receive a coating of mercury in the "quicking" solution preparatory to the plating operation proper.

This method has been termed pyro-plating, and, since its introduction, it has met with great success. Articles of iron or steel are first thoroughly cleansed by filing and scraping them, scouring them in a strong and boiling solution of potash. They are then made the cathode in the same solution, and a very strong current used, which will cause bubbles of gas to arise and make the surface look bright and silvery. They are then placed immediately in the silver plating solution and plated in the usual way.

When the deposit has acquired the desired thickness they are taken out and dried and placed in a furnace and heated. This seems to cause the deposit to enter the pores of the iron or steel and form a kind of alloy at the point of union of the two metals. Should the articles require to be tempered they may be cooled suddenly in water or oil and the proper degree of temper obtained.

PYRO-GILDING is conducted in pretty much the same way, the only difference being that the gold is deposited in successive layers and subjected to heat in the furnace after each coating has been deposited. The operator may be somewhat surprised, when the articles are first heated, at the almost total disappearance of the deposit which has been driven into the pores of the article. The second coating holds its own much better, and the third, or fourth coating, remains entire.

When this operation has been conducted with care, the deposit will be found to be absolutely perfect, and no amount of picking, or chipping at it, will cause it to strip or scale off.

REMEDIES FOR ACCIDENTS.—As the majority of the articles used in electro-plating are more or less poisonous, their different antidotes should be well understood, however, an ounce of pre-. vention is well worth a pound of cure. A careful observance of this old and true maxim by cautiously handling all chemicals and liquids of a poisonous nature will accomplish more good than any or all of the different antidotes, simply by avoiding any occasion for their use.

Cyanide of pottasium is one of the most deadly poisons known, and where a very small quantity of it or any of the cyanide plating solutions have been swallowed death follows almost instantly, there being usually no time to administer antidotes.

Should the patient exhibit signs of life he should be made to swallow a dilute solution of the citrate, acetate or tartrate of iron, and cold water applied to the head and spine, and it should be remembered that whatever is done must be done quickly, as death generally results in a few seconds of time.

During the manufacture of cyanide of potassium and also during the operation for the recovery of metals from cyanide plating solutions. Large volumes of hydro cyanic acid gas is evolved, which is very poisonous and dangerous when inhaled. This may be avoided by conducting the operation in the open air, and where the wind can blow the p)isonous vapors away from the operator. Should the weather or other circumstances arise which would necessitate the operation being conducted in-doors, great care should be taken to secure perfect ventilation.

If either nitric muriatic or sulphuric acid have been swallowed, administer at once an abundance of warm water with a very little mustard in it to serve as an emetic. The anti-dotes are white of eggs, chalk, and water or magnesia and water. Should potash or caustic soda be swallowed, administer lemonade or dilute vinegar.

INDEX.